W9-BRL-231

A RIDE WITH HUEY THE ENGINEER

A RIDE WITH HUEY THE ENGINEER

BY JESSE STUART

ILLUSTRATED BY ROBERT HENNEBERGER

McGraw-Hill Book Company

New York   Toronto   London   Sydney

Also by Jesse Stuart:
ANDY FINDS A WAY
THE BEATINEST BOY
A PENNY'S WORTH OF CHARACTER
RED MULE
THE RIGHTFUL OWNER

Library of Congress Catalog Card Number: AC 66-10456

To my grandnephews

Jefferson Stuart Kirby
James Kraten Kirby
Samuel Lynn Porter
Michael David Abdon
Tony Lee Abdon
Wilfred Eugene Darby
William Thomas Keeney
Lawrence Carroll Keeney
Michael Drew Lake

CONTENTS

CONTENTS

SUNNY'S GREAT DREAM

Sunny Logan lived with his mother and father in a little house which they built themselves of rough boards. The house stood where the road ended at the top of the hill in Clearwater Valley. The soil on this hilly land was poor, and Sunny's parents had to work hard to grow the wheat and potatoes which they needed in order to live. In the spring and summer Sunny helped his parents farm the steep slopes and care for their flock of sheep.

Sunny's father and mother had been born in the area around Clearwater Valley and they had never seen the world beyond the Valley. Their parents were poor and they had to help with the work on the farm and were not able to go to school. But Sunny's parents wanted him to

9

learn to read and write, and when he was six years old they sent him to the Plum Grove School.

Sunny was a happy boy and he was always smiling. He enjoyed talking to the animals and the birds in the surrounding farmlands, and sometimes he even liked talking to himself. He was proud that he was learning to read and write but Sunny had a dream that was even greater than that.

Ever since he could remember, he had dreamed of some day being able to see what lay outside of Clearwater Valley. Every day, for the two years he had been going to school, he would hurry to the tracks just above the Three Mile Station to watch Huey the engineer drive his engine No. 5 along the Eastern Kentucky Railroad. He would not miss seeing Huey for anything in the whole world. Sunny was there at eight every morning when Huey went up the line, and he was back again after school every day to watch the train coast down the grade. Huey the engineer had come to know his young friend and, as he'd drive his train past

Sunny, he'd wave and call to him. Even Ed Webb, the fireman, and Zebo Campbell, the brakeman of the train, recognized Sunny and waved.

But during the summer when Sunny did not go to school, he spent his time working on the farm and caring for the sheep. Often he got lonely and missed going to school. But the thing that Sunny missed most in the world was seeing Huey the engineer.

Sunny could hardly wait for the summer holidays to be over. He was up bright and early on the first day of the new school year. He was eight years old and he was going to be in the third grade.

Sunny's parents knew why he left for school so early in the morning. Everybody in Clearwater Valley knew, and sometimes they teased him about it.

"Where is our boy off to so early?" his mother asked as Sunny strapped his satchel of books over his shoulder and hurried toward the gate of his house. "Don't let Huey the engineer

make you forget your lunch," she called. "You know what's in there today?"

"Wild huckleberry pie," said Sunny as his mother kissed him and stood at the gate watching him run down Clearwater Valley Road, his bare feet leaving tracks in the sand. Sunny always went barefooted everywhere. His feet were tough on the bottoms from farming up in the steep hills, and they were used to the rocks, stumps and briers. Sunny's lunchbox swung back and forth in his hand as he ran. His hair was blond as cornsilks and the summer wind blew it as it blew the silks on the corn.

"I can't be late," Sunny said to himself, but there was no one near to hear him.

He kept on running while a rabbit had to take long hops to get out of his way. A squirrel ran across the road with a walnut in its mouth, then climbed up a tree to its den. But Sunny did not stop for anything. When he turned the bend at the big white oak, a covey of quail flew up in front of him. Even these wild game birds must have wondered why Sunny was in such a hurry, but he was soon out of their sight. As he ran up the sandy road, he looked at the watch on his wrist. He had only seven minutes to get there on time.

At Pop Jackson Hill he overtook a group of his classmates. There was Big Aaron Howard with his little brother Ed and Penny Shelton. Sunny had often passed them on his way to the tracks and he knew they would make jokes as they always did.

"I think I can hear Huey pulling in," shouted Big Aaron. "You'd better pick up speed there, Sunny Logan."

"I wouldn't run like that if a wildcat was after me," laughed Penny Shelton.

But Sunny did not answer his classmates and just hurried on. None of the other children could understand, for no one loved Huey and his train as much as he did.

Sunny turned from the Clearwater Valley Road and followed the path under the persimmon trees, then leaped over a small stream. He passed under a willow grove, then reached the railroad track. Here he stopped and looked at his watch, just as the loud "toot, toot" of a train whistled in the distance.

"I've made it by a minute," he thought. "Huey's just leaving the Three Mile Station."

Sunny put his lunchbox on the ground beside him and removed his satchel from his shoulder. He braced himself against the wind and looked down the track toward Huey's train. The engineer's head was out of the window, and his eyes were on the rusty T-rails. From under his blue

15

and white striped cap his white hair flew in the wind. He was wearing his regular uniform— the blue jumper with white pinstripes to match his cap and the red bandanna around his neck. Clouds of black smoke rose from the train and curled into the August wind.

As the train came closer, Sunny waved both hands and shouted, "Good morning, Huey."

Huey waved back and smiled.

"Good morning, Sunny, my young friend.

We haven't seen you in a very long time."

"It was summer vacation, that's why," shouted Sunny. He hoped that Huey knew how much he had missed him.

Huey was so close now that Sunny could see his white mustache pressed against his face.

Ed Webb, the fireman, was scooping coal into the firebox. He stopped his work for a moment and looked down at Sunny and waved.

The engine chugged, steam hissed from the pistons, and the wheels sent off sparks.

Now Zebo Campbell, the brakeman, saw Sunny. "Good morning, Sunny," he shouted. The big man was riding on the back of the coal tender.

Sunny waved and waved as the train rolled up the track toward the dark mouth of the Barney Tunnel, and he did not stop waving until the train disappeared from sight. He stood for a while looking out in the direction that Huey had gone, then he put his satchel back over his shoulder, lifted his lunchbox and set off to school. He checked his watch and saw that he wouldn't have to hurry to get there on time.

Sunny reached the crossing where the wagon road went down Shacklerun Valley to Plum Grove. He looked up at the sign on the three white boards: STOP-LOOK-LISTEN. Carefully he crossed the tracks, then spotted a yellow and black butterfly. He jumped up to catch it but it flew out of his reach. Then a squirrel with a hickory nut in its mouth crossed Plum Grove Road—Sunny watched it run up a hill, climb a white oak, and vanish into a hole.

"I know where your den is," Sunny said, "but don't be afraid—I won't tell anybody."

When Sunny passed Mr. Wheeler's large farm, with the meadows and cornfields extending as far as his eyes could see, he saw his friend feeding the horses. Sunny had often seen him on his way to school and the old man, who lived alone on the big farm, would always stop Sunny and talk to him. Sunny liked to talk to Mr. Wheeler. But today was the first day of school and there was no time left to stop.

As he ran past the fence of the farm, he heard Mr. Wheeler call, "What's your big hurry?"

Sunny stopped and smiled at his friend. "I
don't want to be late for school, Mr. Wheeler."

The old man watched his horses drink water
from the hollow-log trough. "I'll bet you
waited to see Huey," he said. "Yes, he's a great

engineer. Never had a wreck. Never even hit a dog or a chicken. For fifty years I've been riding to Grayson on his train every Saturday."

Mr. Wheeler's bald head was wet with perspiration. It shone like a pool of water in the sunlight. But he never wore a hat, for he said the sunshine was good for his head, just as it was good for the grass, the corn and the vegetables.

Now he came over to Sunny and tousled his long blond hair.

"And how is my young friend this morning? Glad to be off to school again after the long holiday?"

"Yes," said Sunny. "I'm going to be in the third grade."

"Learning to read and write, eh? And what is my young friend going to be when he grows up?"

Mr. Wheeler had often asked Sunny that question, and Sunny knew it was his way of telling him how important it was to go to school.

"There are so many things I'd like to do," said Sunny. "Like being the engineer of a big train."

Old Mr. Wheeler laughed, and only his gums were showing. "Like good old Huey," he said. "Yes, Huey's a great man—I'll say! Every Saturday all the folk come down from the hills— the men, women and children. They come to see Huey and his engine No. 5. He's a great engineer, that Huey. He used to work as a water boy, then he helped build this railroad. First man ever to drive a train along this Eastern Kentucky Railroad. Now just you keep on going to school, Sunny, and you can be anything that you want to be. When I came to these parts, there wasn't a school around anywhere. So here I am seventy-five years old and I can't read nor write. All the education I ever got I got from experience. I learned when to plant the crops, I raised a family of nine children, and I have saved from this farm over forty thousand dollars. But you, Sunny, are richer than I. You are learning to read and write—and that is the greatest riches you will ever have in the world. You see, I gave the ground from my farm to build the Plum Grove School so good boys like you, Sunny, can get an education."

As the first school bell sounded, Mr. Wheeler tapped Sunny on the forehead.

"Now go along, my young friend, and put riches in that bank above your ears."

Sunny ran beside the fence of Mr. Wheeler's

farm where the vines grew. Here he often stopped to watch the honeybees and butterflies on the yellow blossoms. Then he passed the trees filled with red haws. He liked to gather the ripe haws in his pocket to eat when he got hungry, but today he would let the robins have them, for there was no time to stop.

"Poor Mr. Wheeler," he thought. "He can't even read and write. Maybe I should show him how after Mr. Clarke teaches me."

As Sunny heard the last bell ring, he hurried up the hilltop to the Plum Grove School which stood under a grove of large oaks.

THE FASTEST FOX

Mr. Clarke looked up from his desk when Sunny came into the classroom. He was Sunny's teacher, and he also taught all the grades from the first to the eighth. Sixty boys and girls from the nearby farms in the hills and valleys came to the little one-room school.

"Why are you late this morning?" Mr. Clarke asked Sunny. "Is this a way to begin the new school year?"

"I only stopped to see my friend Mr. Wheeler," said Sunny.

Sunny felt the eyes of all the boys and girls on him, then he saw Big Aaron Howard and Penny Shelton laughing.

"Are you sure Mr. Wheeler didn't stop you?" asked the teacher firmly. "Somebody in

the school has been picking his sweet apples right off his trees. It is one thing to pick the ripe apples off the ground, but you know that Mr. Wheeler has no teeth and he must bake the sweet apples for his breakfast."

"I didn't pick Mr. Wheeler's apples," said Sunny. "I only stopped to talk to him when I saw him watering his horses."

"Well, somebody has. He ran a boy out of his sweet apple tree just the other day."

The classroom turned quiet, and even Big Aaron and Penny Shelton had stopped smiling.

"I want whoever it is that stole the apples to come up before the classroom and tell the truth."

Mr. Clarke looked down the two aisles of girls and boys but no one moved from his desk.

"Very well," he said. "Sunny, you may take your seat." Sternly he started the lesson.

When recess came, Mr. Clarke announced that he had brought his barbering tools along that day. There were no barber shops in the area and many of the farmers couldn't cut their sons' hair, so Mr. Clarke bought himself a set of tools and decided to act as barber to his pupils. But that wasn't all that Mr. Clarke did. Since his pupils came to school barefooted, he also brought needles to remove the briers from their feet and medicine for cuts and bruises.

Big Aaron was the first to reach the tree stump which Mr. Clarke used as his barber's chair. The teacher put an apron around Big Aaron's neck and got to work on his long dark hair with his hand clippers and scissors. Penny Shelton and some of the other boys had already lined up, but Sunny was not among them.

When Mr. Clarke had finished with Big Aaron, he looked around, then he saw Sunny's long blond hair blowing in the wind.

"Sunny," he called, "I think you should be next."

"Please, Mr. Clarke," said Sunny, "don't cut my hair."

"But you said the same thing last year too.

It looks to me like your hair hasn't been cut all summer long."

Big Aaron, who was proud of his new short haircut, tapped Penny Shelton on the shoulder, and they both laughed as though they knew Sunny's secret.

"But, Sunny," said the teacher, "why do you insist on keeping your hair so long?"

"Do you suppose it's because of Huey the engineer?" burst in Big Aaron, and the two boys laughed even louder.

The teacher looked coldly at Big Aaron. "If that happens once again, I'll have to keep you after school."

Big Aaron's expression changed very fast, and he and his little brother Ed and Penny Shelton walked off into the playground.

"But it's true what he said," Sunny told his teacher. "I want to be a big engineer like Huey someday—and that's how Huey wears his hair. Have you ever seen it blow on the wind when he pulls No. 5 up the tracks?"

"Yes, Huey is a fine man," said Mr. Clarke with a smile. "All right, Sunny. I'll wait just a little while longer before cutting your hair."

During the noon hour, the Plum Grove boys played fox and hound. Sunny was the fastest and best runner, so he was chosen to be the fox. They played on the pasture fields and woodlands which belonged to Mr. Wheeler.

Sunny, the fox, was allowed to start three hundred feet ahead of the hounds. Big Aaron, who had had his hair cut short so the wind wouldn't hold him back, wanted to be the first hound to catch Sunny Logan.

As the fox chase began, the Plum Grove girls stopped playing London Bridge and watched. They saw Sunny Logan running, with his long hair riding on the wind. And right behind was Big Aaron, the hound, chasing Sunny over the pasture toward the woodlands. Suddenly Big Aaron bent over and stopped, but the other foxhounds kept on going, for they knew a good hound never left the chase.

Big Aaron watched the others head past him, then he turned and went limping back toward the schoolhouse.

"Look what's in my foot," he said to Mr.

Clarke as he sat down on a nearby tree stump.

Big Aaron had run a honey-locust thorn into his foot, and Mr. Clarke sent one of the girls to get the first-aid kit.

"It will hurt," Mr. Clarke told Big Aaron as he removed a pair of tweezers from his kit. "But don't holler if you can help it."

Big Aaron closed his eyes and tightened his lips as Mr. Clarke struggled to get the thorn out.

When he finally got it, he held up the long thorn.

"It is easier to pull a tooth," he said, "than a thorn that has gone all the way into a foot." Mr. Clarke applied some medicine to the foot, then wrapped a bandage around it. "Now go sit down in the schoolhouse and rest your foot for a while."

But Big Aaron did not move from the tree stump on which he sat. He just looked at his teacher with a strange expression on his face. "Mr. Clarke," he said after a while, "there is something I must tell you. Sunny is not to blame. I am the one who has been picking Mr. Wheeler's sweet apples."

"It is important that you have told me the truth. Of course, you will stay behind after school this afternoon."

Big Aaron lifted himself from the tree stump and limped back toward the schoolhouse. He had just reached the first step when Sunny, the fox, came running across the pasture with not a single hound in sight.

AN INVITATION FROM HUEY

As Sunny stood waiting for Huey's train a few days later, No. 5 engine panted slowly up the track, throwing clouds of smoke into the air.

"He's not got much speed this morning," thought Sunny. "There must be something wrong."

When the train reached Sunny, it stopped. The smiling face of Huey looked down. He had on his blue and white striped cap and the red bandanna around his neck.

"Hello, my young friend," he called. "Did you have a good summer?"

"I'm glad it's school again so I can see your train."

"You've never missed a day, have you?"

"Oh, no," said Sunny.

"And I don't even think you've ever ridden my train," shouted Huey.

"No, sir, I never have," replied Sunny. "I've never ridden on any train."

"Well, young man, don't you think it's time you climbed up here in the engine and rode with me to the end of the line?"

Sunny could hardly speak for a moment. "That would be the greatest thing that ever happened to me," he said dreamily.

"Then you go home and ask your mom and dad. If they say yes, wait for me Saturday morning at the Three Mile Station."

Huey pulled on his throttle. Engine No. 5 sent up clouds of smoke, and the train started rolling up the tracks.

"I'm going to see the world!" called Sunny as he jumped high in the air and clapped his hands. He waved at the passengers as the coach went by. "On Saturday I'm going to be up there like you," he shouted, "and Huey the engineer will show me everything."

When Sunny ran up the hill to the schoolhouse, Big Aaron came right up to him.

"What makes you so happy this morning?" he asked Sunny.

"You won't believe it when I tell you," said Sunny. "Huey the engineer just stopped his train and invited me to ride with him to the end of the line."

Big Aaron began laughing. With a sweep of his hand he called the other boys and girls over. Soon there was a big circle around Sunny Logan.

"Now you tell them what you told me," said Big Aaron.

"Huey invited me to go for a ride in engine No. 5," said Sunny proudly. "He wants me to ride up in the engine with him."

The boys and girls laughed, and no one believed that Sunny was telling the truth.

"That Sunny Logan has been having strange dreams," said Big Aaron, and the children laughed even louder.

Mr. Clarke heard the noise. "What's going on here?" he asked as he joined the circle gathered around Sunny Logan.

"Tell him," said Big Aaron. "Let us hear you tell him too!"

"They don't believe me," Sunny told his teacher, "but it's true that Huey the engineer is taking me for a ride to the end of the line."

Mr. Clarke did not seem surprised at all. He looked around the circle of boys and girls, and slowly their laughing faces disappeared.

"Why shouldn't Huey take Sunny for a ride in his train?" the teacher asked. "If any boy in this class deserves to travel and see the world, it is Sunny Logan."

At morning recess, Big Aaron came over to Sunny and said he was sorry he hadn't believed him at first.

"Do you think I can come along also?" he asked.

"Maybe you should come with me to Huey's train after school and ask him," said Sunny.

Big Aaron said he wasn't sure he could come, and walked off with his little brother to join Penny Shelton.

Sunny was happier than he had ever been in his life. His face was beaming and he could not help smiling when he thought of his journey with Huey.

At noon, when the boys played fox and hound again, Sunny ran across the pasture, chugging like Huey's No. 5 engine. He left behind all the hounds, and as he reached the schoolhouse he made two short whistles, which meant that he should stop.

Sunny couldn't wait to see Huey again that afternoon. As soon as school was over, he asked Big Aaron if he wanted to come but his classmate had already changed his mind. Sunny put his satchel over his shoulder, took his lunchbox, and hurried down the road. As he passed the red haw bushes, he saw the robins in the branches gathering the ripest haws. The pawpaw bushes and persimmon trees were laden with ripe fruit too, but today Sunny was too excited to stop and gather the fruit. He waved to Mr. Wheeler as he saw him forking the windrows of hay, then went straight toward the railroad track to wave to Huey.

When Sunny came home that afternoon, he found his mother and father in the garden picking vegetables. As he ran toward his mother, she stopped gathering the beans from the vines and smiled at her happy son. Her eyes were as blue as Sunny's and her hair was blond as the cornsilks.

"Guess what happened today," said Sunny with excitement.

"Did my boy get the best mark in school?"

"No," said Sunny, "something even greater."

Sunny's father, who was on the other side of the garden putting the ripe tomatoes into baskets, saw Sunny jumping with happiness. "What is all the excitement?" he called.

"Try to guess!" shouted Sunny.

His father lifted two baskets of tomatoes and came over.

"I have no idea," he said. "Do you, Mary?" he asked Sunny's mother.

"Well," she said, "since it isn't the best mark, maybe our boy got the prize for always coming to school on time."

"No," said Sunny, "something even greater than that!"

"Greater?" said his father. "I can't imagine

what that could be—unless perhaps you were fox today and beat all the hounds."

Sunny laughed up at his father. "No, Dad, you know that happens every day. Guess again!"

His father looked down at him curiously. "I cannot imagine what it could be. It's not the best mark in school. It's not the prize for always coming on time. And now you say it's not for being the fastest fox. And still you expect me to guess?" He turned to Sunny's mother, whose eyes were sparkling as much as her son's. "Can there be anything else, Mary?"

"Well, if there is, I sure can't imagine what it could be, Bill," she answered.

"Just try once more!" said Sunny.

"Well," said his mother thinking hard, "maybe it has to do with Mr. Wheeler?"

"No!"

"I know," said his father suddenly, "Sunny found a squirrel's den today."

"No!"

"Sunny found a tree with honeybees!"

"No," laughed Sunny.

"Then I give up," said his father. "Do you, Mary?"

"I don't know what else I can do," said Sunny's mother.

"All right," said Sunny, "I'll tell you both. But promise that you will believe me?"

"Of course we'll believe our boy," said Sunny's mother.

"Well, nobody else did," said Sunny. "Only Mr. Clarke believed me."

"I wonder what it is," Sunny's father said in amazement.

"All right, I'll tell you," said Sunny. "But will you say yes?"

Sunny's mother and father looked at each other. "If it is reasonable, Sunny, then we surely will."

"It's very reasonable," said Sunny. "And it's also the greatest thing that happened in my whole life." He stared up at his mother and father and they saw that his eyes were full of wonder and happiness. "Huey the engineer is taking me for a ride in his train. This morning he invited me. This morning he stopped the train and invited me."

Sunny's parents looked at each other. "Stopped the train?" his father said.

"And he's taking me to the end of the line," said Sunny, jumping up and down in excitement. "And you know what else? It's not in the passenger car like all the other people. I'm going to ride right up in the engine with Huey!"

Sunny's parents looked so surprised that Sunny couldn't stop laughing.

"So can I go?" shouted Sunny.

"Imagine," said his father, "Huey, the great engineer!"

"So can I?" shrieked Sunny, staring up at his father in joy.

"It looks to me," said Sunny's mother, "like our boy is about to see more of the world than his parents ever have."

THE BIG RIDE

That Saturday Sunny was up at five o'clock in the morning. He helped his father feed the horses and milk the cows, then he and his mother and father sat down for breakfast. Since it was still dark, they ate by lamplight.

After breakfast Sunny changed into the new overalls and blue shirt which his mother had made him especially for his trip. Although Sunny was the only boy in Plum Grove School whose mother made his clothes, he did not mind, and today he felt very proud of his new outfit.

"How nice you look this morning," his mother said. "But, Sunny, don't you think your hair is getting a little too long?"

"Mary," said Sunny's father, "you know that our boy wants to look just like Huey the engineer."

49

"Huey's hair is even longer," said Sunny. "Did you ever see how it flies in the wind when he drives in his engine No. 5?"

Sunny's parents smiled at each other and wished him a happy journey as he left the little plank house at the top of the high hill. He swung his lunchbox happily and held the package with the wild huckleberry pie his mother

had made especially for Huey. Sunny looked back and waved to his mother and father, who were standing at the gate, then he walked down the narrow road, watching the tracks his feet left in the sand.

He had not gone far when he saw a mother quail crossing the road, with her eleven little quails following. As she saw Sunny coming, she rose into the air and flew over the fence into a cornfield. There was a loud fluttering of wings as her eleven little quails went after her.

"I, too, am going far away," said Sunny to the mother quail. "I'm going off on a train."

The quails made a loud sound and Sunny smiled and wondered whether they really understood.

A rabbit hopped across the road in front of him.

"I'm not going to chase after you," said Sunny. "Right now I'm going to ride with Huey the engineer and see the world."

Clearwater Valley had always looked beautiful to Sunny. So often on his way to school in the morning he had seen the sun rise, and he had seen it set over the high range of hills when he returned home from school. But somehow today the sunrise looked more beautiful than ever before, and the dew on the blades of corn and meadow grass sparkled like a million jewels. The song of the birds rose into the air.

As the sun came out, the butterflies and honeybees began flying from blossom to blossom to find a breakfast of sweet nectar. Everywhere that Sunny looked there were morning-glory bells of every color filled with honey bees and butterflies.

Then he saw the squirrel with the hickory nut in his mouth going toward his den. Sunny told the squirrel about his big trip, then ran across the fields toward the Three Mile Station.

When Sunny reached the station there was no one in sight. It was only seven-thirty, and Huey's train would not be pulling in until eight o'clock.

As he waited, he saw Mr. Wheeler coming down the tracks, carrying a large willow basket. He was going to Grayson, as he did every Saturday, to sell the fresh butter and eggs. Mr.

Wheeler was wearing his corduroy suit and heavy coat, and his bald head shone in the morning sun.

"Good morning, my young friend," he said as he saw Sunny. "Where are you going this lovely Saturday morning?"

"I am going all the way to the end of the line with Huey," said Sunny proudly.

"All the way to Webbville!" said Mr. Wheeler. "That's even farther than I have ever ridden with Huey. Often I have wondered what Webbville was like."

"Even my mother and father have wondered. They've never seen the world," said Sunny.

"I'm only going as far as Grayson," said Mr. Wheeler. "But if you don't mind, my young friend, I would like to sit together in the coach with you."

Sunny laughed with happiness. "I'm not riding in the coach, Mr. Wheeler," he said. "I'm riding up in the engine with Huey."

54

Mr. Wheeler looked straight at Sunny. "Now what did you say?"

"That's right," Sunny laughed. "I'm riding right up in the engine. Huey stopped his train and invited me. I've never missed seeing Huey a day."

Mr. Wheeler made a sound with his throat. "I'll say, my young friend is going places!" He tousled Sunny's hair and laughed.

Just then they heard a train whistle.

"Listen!" said Sunny. "That's Huey coming."

The smoke came puffing up in dark clouds and Sunny ran down the cinder path beside the track. As the train came nearer, Sunny could see Huey's head out of the cab window. His blue and white striped cap kept the morning wind from blowing his long white hair, and the red bandanna was wrapped around his neck. There was a smile on his face when he looked down at Sunny, who ran beside the engine until it stopped.

"Good morning, Sunny," he shouted. "You are here on time."

"Yes, sir," said Sunny. "I was the first one here."

Huey greeted Mr. Wheeler, and Conductor McKee put a footstool down for Mr. Wheeler to step up on. Then he walked briskly into the passenger coach, shouting good morning to everyone.

"Now, Sunny, come right up on," said Huey.

Sunny ran up the steps between the coal tender and the engine and looked down at the passengers who were hurrying to make the train. A lady screamed, "Don't start yet! They're coming!" and a group of women and children came running behind her.

"All right, folks, we'll wait," called Huey. "But, remember, our train must be on time."

Ed Webb, the fireman, told Sunny to sit beside him. "The engineer must sit by himself," he said. "He must keep his hand on the throttle and his eye on the rail. Right, Huey?"

"Right!"

Huey looked back as Conductor McKee gave him the signal to start.

"We'll be going upgrade all the way," Ed
Webb told Sunny. "But you'll be able to see
everything from the window."

Sunny was too busy watching Huey to look out of the window. He studied the brakes and gadgets while Ed Webb scooped coal into the firebox. Zebo Campbell, the brakeman, was riding on the coal tender alongside Ed Webb.

When Huey pulled the throttle back, the engine chugged harder and faster. The big drive wheels spun on the rusty rails and clouds of black smoke rolled into the sky.

"Now watch old No. 5 get down and pull," said Ed Webb. "With that throttle, Huey can get every ounce of strength from his engine."

The train rolled up the tracks and swirled past the cornfields, meadows and country roads that were so familiar to Sunny. Then it seemed to lurch around and up Ferguson Curve toward the Barney Tunnel.

"Have you ever gone through the tunnel?" Ed Webb asked Sunny.

"Never."

"Huey turns the headlights on in the tunnels," Ed Webb told him. "We'll also cross twenty-two bridges. We'll cross the Little

Sandy River four times, the Little Fork seven times, and Dry Fork four times. Then we cross seven other streams."

Huey reached up and pulled a gadget, all the while keeping his hand on the throttle and his eyes on the rails.

"Did Huey just put the headlights on?" asked Sunny.

"I'll tell you, Sunny," said Ed Webb, "this electricity is wonderful stuff. In the old days we had to use kerosene lamps, and that was no easy thing."

"In we go!" shouted Sunny as the train went into the tunnel.

The engine panted and clouds of coal smoke swirled back past Sunny's window. Then the sound of the engine changed and it began to grow lighter as the train came back into the daylight. Huey reached up and pulled a cord, and a long, lonely whistle sounded far over the hilly farms.

"Right now men and women everywhere are stopping their work and setting their watches with that whistle," said Ed Webb.

"Huey's known all the way up and down the Eastern Kentucky Railroad, and never once has he been late."

As they passed through Nellavale, the mail clerk hooked a mailbag that was hanging near the train and pulled it into the baggage car, then threw another mailbag onto the station.

"Old Lafe is a good mail clerk," said Ed. "He's been on this train for years."

"He's as fast as a hornet pouncing on a fly!" laughed Sunny.

The train ran across a narrow valley between two hills.

"In a minute we'll be going into the McIntire Tunnel," said Ed. "It's only a short one. The tunnels along this line in Greenup County are as thick as lightning bugs on a warm June night."

The train screaked around a curve between high stone walls, passed through the tunnel and popped out on the other side of McIntire Hill. Vast cornfields lay bathed in the bright morning light.

Huey sounded the long, lonely whistle and

the train rushed onto an iron bridge looking down over the East Fork River.

"We're riding high and fast," said Sunny, looking down over the river. "I'm so high up I'd hate to fall all the way down."

Suddenly Huey made two short whistles and the train began to slow down.

"Where are we coming to now?" asked Sunny.

"I don't know why Huey is stopping," said Ed. As he and Sunny looked out of the window, they saw two hunters.

"Sorry to stop you, Huey," they said as the engine slowed down beside them, "but we've just got out of the woods and we didn't have time to get to Simonton and up to Argillite."

"All right, boys," said Huey. "Get on the vestibule but see that the shells are out of your guns."

"No squirrels out here," said one of the men. "We're headed for Hopewell to try the Big Woods. Hear there are plenty up there cutting on the hickory nuts."

The two men paid their fares to the conductor, and the engine panted and rattled as the train started. In a few minutes it pulled into Argillite.

Passengers were getting on and off the train, and there was a crowd of men, women and children who had come from the hills especially to see Huey and to speak to him. Huey knew everyone, and he called each person by his first name.

As Ed Webb scooped more coal into the coal tender, Zebo Campbell gave Huey the signal, and slowly the train moved away from the station. Huey waved to all his friends who remained standing as old No. 5 went up the grade toward the Argillite Tunnel.

"Did all those people come to see Huey?" asked Sunny.

"Every Saturday they take a holiday and come down from the hills and hollows to greet Huey and old No. 5. For most of them, this is the only train they've ever seen. And everybody loves Huey. He was the first engineer to drive a train along this Eastern Kentucky Railroad."

Ed Webb put his coal scoop back on the coal tender and wiped his hot face with his soiled bandanna. Then he sat down beside Sunny.

"We leave day and go into night!" shouted Sunny as Huey pulled into the Argillite Tunnel. "We're going to come out on the other side of the hill in a few minutes, and it will be daylight again."

"I'll say it will," said Ed Webb. "Huey makes his run from one end of the track to the other in three hours. Just think, thirty-six miles in three hours!"

"Whew!" said Sunny.

"Huey has been an engineer for fifty years,"

said Ed Webb. "He used to work as a water boy. Later he helped build this railroad."

"No wonder Huey is such a great man," said Sunny as he watched Huey in admiration.

Suddenly Zebo Campbell came running in from the passenger car and signaled Huey to stop the train. "There's a fight there on the passenger coach," he announced. "Some Argillite rowdies wanted an audience to settle their troubles."

As Huey stopped the train, Zebo Campbell ran back and threw them off.

"When they don't know how to behave, let them try walking," Huey said as he started up the train.

Sunny looked back and saw three young men standing on the tracks and shaking their fists up at Zebo Campbell, who stood on the vestibule.

"These young rowdies have often stoned the train coming out of a tunnel," said Ed Webb. "They stand on the high ledges and throw rocks down. But Zebo takes care of them. He runs out on the vestibule and makes the bullets sing all around them. And that scares the rowdies off!"

Huey pulled the train through three other tunnels, then passed an old coal field with big dumps of blue slate and ugly dark holes on the rough hill slopes. Coal tipples still stood at the mouths of many of the mines.

"This was once considered the greatest coal field in this country, but it didn't last. The coal was hard and didn't leave cinders when it burned."

The train rushed past the fields, then Huey sounded his whistle as he neared the Hunnewell Station.

"Huey's pulling into his old home town now," said Ed Webb. "Hunnewell used to be a big place when Huey lived there. The hills were full of coal and iron ore, and over five hundred people lived there. Now all that is left is a railroad station, a church, a store and a dozen houses. But Huey is not forgotten. Every Saturday his old friends gather in the station to greet him. They come from the Little Sandy Valley, from Cane Creek and Turkey Lick and some from the ridges too. Look, Sunny—see the big crowd gathered there!"

"I never saw so many people," said Sunny.

Everyone swarmed around the train as Huey slowed down and stopped.

"Welcome back, Huey," said an old woman.

"Thank you, Nellie," said Huey. "It's always good to get back to Hunnewell."

They all tried to speak to Huey at the same time. Those who didn't have a chance just smiled and waved.

Conductor McKee took care of the passengers and Lafe O'Bryan exchanged mailbags with the Hunnewell postmaster. Zebo Campbell was loading the freight into the train, then he gave Huey the signal to start. The crowd waved and cheered until the train was out of sight.

When Huey neared the Big Tunnel, the longest on the Eastern Kentucky Railroad, something hit the top of the engine, and Huey blew the whistle six times.

"Keep your head inside the window," Ed Webb warned Sunny. "The rowdies are throwing rocks down from that high hill again."

More rocks were coming down on the train.

"I see them up there," said Sunny. "They look like real bandits with those handkerchiefs over their faces."

"Don't worry, Zebo will take care of them," said Ed Webb.

Boom! Boom! Boom! Boom! The shots came
faster than Sunny could count.

"They're running," said Sunny. "They're
getting behind cliffs."

"They'd better get behind something," said
Ed Webb. "Zebo can shoot close enough to
scare them to death."

More shots were coming from the baggage
coach.

"When they stone a mail train, they're fooling with Uncle Sam," Ed Webb said. "Mail has
to go through and Lafe O'Bryan carries a pistol
and a Winchester. Hear him now!"

As Lafe O'Bryan shot toward the cliffs, the men quickly disappeared from sight.

The train crossed over the Sandy River Bridge, passed through Hopewell Station and Greenup and Carter Counties. It passed the rolling hills where sheep and cattle grazed, and sped through the fertile valleys with their fields of corn.

"Now we come to the bridges," said Ed Webb. "Plenty of them. But we need more steam. Huey's been bearing down on that whistle a lot."

Ed Webb opened the door to the firebox with a long hook and began scooping coal on the leaping flames.

Sunny looked down from his window where the railroad followed the Sandy River and saw two boys with fishing poles sitting in a small boat. The boys took off their straw hats and waved to the train. Sunny waved back to them as the train went around a sharp curve and the wheels screaked against the rusty T-rails.

"Pactolus! Pactolus!" shouted Conductor McKee as the train pulled into the station.

72

Some passengers were leaving the coach and others were getting on. As Huey left the station, he moved faster across the level Sandy River Valley, then suddenly he put the brake on and blew his whistle again and again.

"What's the trouble?" called Ed Webb as he and Sunny looked out of the window.

A flock of sheep stood on the tracks and refused to move.

"Ed, you'll have to go down and shoo them off," said Huey.

"We have sheep at home," said Sunny, "and I know how to get them off. May I go?"

Huey smiled broadly. "All right, Sunny. Let's see you shoo them off."

Sunny got off the train and walked among the flock until he came to an old ewe wearing a bell. He took her by the collar and slowly led her off the track. Her bell tingled and her flock followed.

"Well done, Sunny!" Huey said as Sunny climbed back into the engine. He pulled the throttle and chugged off toward Grayson.

"Now we're coming to the biggest town along the E.K.," said Ed Webb. "Grayson must have over fifteen hundred people!"

"Fifteen hundred!" Sunny was amazed.

"Old No. 5 pulled the bricks here to build the

houses. It was hard work for the engine, but now they've built a big town with the bricks. Saturday morning this coach is loaded with people going to Grayson to trade their eggs and butter at the stores for groceries and notions."

When the train pulled into Grayson, Mr. Wheeler was the first to get off. He took long steps as he walked down the street crowded with people.

"Good-bye, Mr. Wheeler!" shouted Sunny.

The old farmer turned back and smiled and waved at Sunny who was sitting up in the engine.

"Good-bye, my young friend," he shouted. "See you again at the Three Mile Station."

The train left Grayson and crossed a bridge over Little Sandy.

"Huey is going to fly now," said Ed Webb. "The track is straight and level. No tunnels in Carter County. We follow the rivers and cross the bridges."

As they sped across another bridge, Ed Webb said, "We leave Little Sandy now. It goes one way and we go another. Now we follow Little Fork."

Sunny counted seven bridges across Little Fork. The train passed the flagstops at Reedville and Butler, then stopped at a water tank. When they reached Willard Station, a large crowd was gathered there.

"This used to be another big town," said Ed Webb. "When the coal mines were doing well, there used to be over six hundred people here. Now the coal is playing out and there are not more than two hundred people left."

The train moved on and soon Ed Webb announced that they were reaching the end of the line. "It won't be long now," he said. "We'll soon leave Carter County and enter Lawrence County. Ever hear of it, Sunny?"

"Yes, I have."

Sunny counted five more bridges over Dry Fork. "Just think," he said, "through Greenup and Carter Counties and into Lawrence in only three hours! We sure have been flying!"

"Now we're pulling into Webbville," said Ed Webb. "The end of the line."

Sunny's eyes widened and a large smile spread across his face. "I've seen the world," he said, "and I'll never forget it."

Huey looked at his watch and smiled. Then he stood up and raised his arms above his head. "We're on time," he said. "How did you like your ride, Sunny?"

Sunny's face beamed as he looked at Huey. "It is the greatest trip I have ever taken in my whole life—and the first one. Today I have seen things that even my mother and father haven't, and when I get home I'll have lots and lots of things to tell them about the world."

"You certainly will, young man," said Huey with a wink. "Now you come up on the station platform with me and we'll have our lunch. Ed stays with No. 5 while the master mechanic checks it at noon."

Sunny followed Huey, who was carrying his lunch and also a large cardboard box. Sunny brought along the lunch that his mother had prepared, and they both sat down on the long seat on the platform.

"I see you have brought along your own

lunch," said Huey. "What am I going to do with the food I packed especially for you?"

"And I have brought along something special for you too, Huey. I went to the hills to pick huckleberries so my mother could make wild huckleberry pie."

Sunny opened his package and took out the pie that his mother had made especially for Huey.

"Huckleberry pie!" said Huey. "How did you know just what I was wishing for? Thank you, my young friend. Thank you very much. Now won't you try one of my sandwiches?"

Sunny took the sandwich happily and began eating.

"Do you think I can learn to drive a train some day?" he asked the engineer. "That is what I have always wanted to be—a great engineer like you, Huey."

Huey laughed as he looked at Sunny. "I think there's a chance," he said. "Why don't you take a peek inside that box?"

Sunny looked at the large cardboard box that lay beside him.

"Go on," said Huey, "open it up and let us see what's inside."

Sunny was full of excitement as he untied the box. Huey was watching him and his face was wrinkled with smiles. First Sunny pulled out a blue and white striped cap. Then there were the overalls and jumper to match. Bursts of excitement sprang from him as he pulled out the red bandanna and a pair of shoes.

"It's just like yours, Huey," he shrieked with joy. He held the clothes against him. "I'm a big engineer now!"

"Try it on," said Huey. "Let's see how you look in your uniform."

Sunny was so happy he could not speak. He looked from Huey to the present and his face was beaming.

"It's your present from the crew," said Huey. "Ed Webb, Zebo Campbell and me."

"Can I put it on now?" said Sunny. "I want to wear it instead of my real clothes. Can I wear it back on the train to the Three Mile Station?"

"That's just what I had in mind," said Huey, smiling at Sunny and rumpling his long blond hair.

"I didn't have my hair cut," said Sunny, "so I could be a big engineer like you."

Huey laughed. "Now have your lunch, young man. There'll be plenty of time for you to get into your uniform."

———◆———

HOME AGAIN

At one-thirty the train was ready to leave. Sunny, in his new uniform, climbed up the steps behind Huey and looked like one of the crew. His long blond hair hung under his cap just like Huey's.

"Sunny, you'll be helping me out on the return trip," said Huey. "We'll both take the driver's seat and keep our hands on the throttle and our eyes on the rails."

"Help you out?" Sunny stared at Huey to see if he was serious. Then he quickly took his position at the driver's seat.

"Ease out on the throttle," said Huey as his trained hand guided Sunny's.

The engine began to move down the line and Sunny could feel the great power at his fingertips. His face was beaming and his lips were

curved in a broad smile. His hair was flying like
Huey's. The Lawrence County hills and the
telephone poles swirled by, and they raced
through Bellstrace with a long trail of smoke fol-

lowing. They crossed from Lawrence to Carter County with the whistle screaming. People stopped their work in the fields to look up and wave.

They stopped at Lost Spur to pick up a carload of coal.

"We'll have a long train going down," said Huey. "We've got two more cars to pick up."

They moved swiftly down the line, crossing bridges and waving to people. Huey let the engine's big brass bell ring all the way into Willard, where they stopped again. Below Willard they came to John Creek's spur, where they added two more cars of coal to the train. Then they moved through Butler and Reedsville. They stopped in Hitchens to load and unload the freight, then moved over the flat valley where the wheels sang a tune on the rusted rails. They crossed more bridges with the whistle screaming and the bell ringing. When they pulled into Grayson, Sunny saw Mr. Wheeler with his basket waiting amid the crowd. But Mr. Wheeler did not see Sunny up in the driver's seat, as he was too busy trying to get a seat in the coach.

A passenger asked Huey, "Is that your grandson up there?"

"He's my friend," said Huey. "He's on his way to becoming a real engineer."

Sunny sat proudly on the seat and nodded to the man.

When all the passengers were in the coach, Conductor McKee signaled the train to move on.

"Easy on the throttle," said Huey.

The two engineers eased the throttle and the train moved along. Ed Webb scooped more coal into the firebox and Zebo Campbell rode up on the freight car as the train thundered and screaked down the tracks. They passed fields with horses, sheep and herds of cattle.

"Now we must go slow down this grade to make the Anglin Curve," said Huey. "This train is long enough to jump the tracks."

They screaked slowly around the track that curved with the Sandy River. People were fishing from little boats. They looked up as the train rolled past and they waved with their hats and their handkerchiefs.

When they reached Hopewell, Zebo Campbell left the freight car and came back to his old
seat in the engine. "I don't want to get my head
knocked off in that Hopewell Tunnel," he told
Ed Webb.

Sunny jerked his head back as they dove into
the tunnel.

Huey laughed. "I know how you feel, Sunny. I did that when I first pulled my train through the Barney Tunnel. But a good engineer must always keep his eyes on the rails."

"That's what I'll do," said Sunny.

The train leaped on, and now Sunny was passing through tunnels without even blinking an eye. He felt so wonderful that he laughed loudly when the train thundered through darkness and came into daylight again.

Further along the tracks they were flagged by Ott Willis, the greatest fox hunter in those parts, who had his six hounds with him.

"I'll declare," he said when he saw Sunny. "Could that be Bill and Mary Logan's boy up there with you?" he asked Huey.

"That is right," said Huey.

"Is he by any chance going to take over old No. 5?"

"I'm not about to argue that point," said Huey with a special wink at his young engineer.

The train flew through tunnels at Shelton, Ramey and Callihan, but after it passed through the Argillite Tunnel Sunny grew a little sad. "We only have two more tunnels left before we reach Three Mile."

"You just keep up the good work, my young friend, and you'll be running No. 5 without old Huey!"

The whistle screamed and the bell rang and the engine tried to outrun the ribbon of smoke that followed. They went through the McIntire Tunnel and across the high hill over Nellavale. Then engine No. 5 rounded a curve and entered the Barney Tunnel. Sunny was coming back home again to the hills, meadows and valleys that were so familiar to him.

When they pulled into the Three Mile Station, Huey rose and congratulated Sunny. "You're a young engineer, all right," he said.

"You have handled old No. 5 like an expert."

Ed Webb, Zebo Campbell, Conductor Mc-
Kee and even Lafe O'Bryan gathered around
Sunny. They all wanted him to come back
soon again.

"I'll be back," said Sunny. "I'm not even
going to take off my uniform."

He leaped off the train, laughing happily,
and right before him stood Mr. Wheeler.

"Are old Wheeler's eyes fooling him?" said
the farmer. "I thought you were my friend
Huey."

"I'm an engineer now," said Sunny, looking
up at Mr. Wheeler. "Huey bought me the uniform and he let me drive with him all the way
back to Three Mile."

"Then I think I know who is going to take
old Wheeler to the Grayson market next Saturday."

"You can depend on me!" said Sunny.

No. 5 threw up puffs of smoke and the crew
stood up and waved and smiled at Sunny as the
train pulled away.

"I must hurry," Sunny said to Mr. Wheeler.

"Everybody is waiting to hear all about the big world."

The farmer watched Sunny run off into the fields toward his home. "If I hadn't seen it with my own eyes," Mr. Wheeler said, "I could have bet my fresh eggs and butter that the little fellow there in the uniform was my old friend Huey."

———————◆———————

About the Author and Artist

Jesse Stuart is the popular author of such books as ANDY FINDS A WAY, THE BEATINEST BOY, A PENNY'S WORTH OF CHARACTER, RED MULE and THE RIGHTFUL OWNER. Like his many books for grownups, these have earned the highest critical praise throughout the country. He has won many awards, prizes, and fellowships. He also received the annual $5,000 award of the Academy of American Poets "for distinguished poetic achievement."

Mr. Stuart was born in W-Hollow near Greenup, Kentucky, where he still lives. He went to a one-room Kentucky school much like the one in this story. After graduating from high school, he worked his way through college, and then did graduate work at Vanderbilt University and Peabody College.

At seventeen he started teaching in a rural schoolhouse, and he eventually became superintendent of various city and county schools in Kentucky.

Robert Henneberger has already won great acclaim for his illustrations in Jesse Stuart's earlier books and many other books for children. Born in Baltimore, he grew up more interested in drawing pictures than in other childhood activities. After the war, he graduated from Rhode Island School of Design, settled in Providence with his wife, and started his career as an illustrator.